A Lift-the-Flap Book

Pete the Cat

The First Thanksgiving

Kimberly & James Dean

Pete was nervous about being a Pilgrim in his class's Thanksgiving play, *The First Thanksgiving*.

"Just do your best," his best friend, Callie, said.

Pete the Cat

The First Thanksgiving

Kimberly & James Dean

Pete was nervous about being a Pilgrim in his class's Thanksgiving play, *The First Thanksgiving.*
"Just do your best," his best friend, Callie, said.

HAPPY THANKSGIVING!

Pete said he would try. He was ready. His mom had even made him a pilgrim hat, which was really cool.

Pete took his place at the front of the giant ship that his class had made out of cardboard. Pete was a Pilgrim on the *Mayflower*.

The dream of a new start in a New World made the hard trip all worth it. For more than two months the Pilgrims sailed.

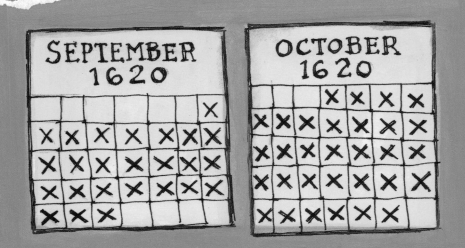

SEPTEMBER 1620

OCTOBER 1620

NOVEMBER 1620

In 1620, a group of Pilgrims decided to leave England for the New World to build a new life.

"It was a long, long trip on a big, big ship!" all the Pilgrims sang.

LAND, HO!

After sixty-five days on the ship, the New World finally came into view.

The Pilgrims arrived in the New World at Plymouth Rock in what is now Massachusetts. Everyone had many chores to do, like growing food, finding water . . .

The first winter in the New World was long and hard.

The Pilgrims had heard about the Native Americans, and many worried that they would not be friendly. Pete had never met a cat he didn't like, so he thought they would be kind.

Pete was right. He made a new friend in Squanto. Squanto and the other Native Americans showed the Pilgrims how to grow crops like corn, beans, and squash.

By fall harvest, the Pilgrims had plenty of food.
To thank Squanto and the other Native Americans, the
Pilgrims invited them to share the harvest.

Pete was relieved when the play was over. He had remembered all his lines!

"Wow, I never thought about how hard it was back then," said Pete.

Later, at Thanksgiving dinner with his family, Pete said, "Let's all go around the table and say something we are thankful for."